Royally Enchanted

CARTOON TALES

Royally Enchanted

CARTOON TALES

ADAPTED BY SCOTT PETERSON

Disney PRESS

New York

Artwork for *Cinderella* by Mario Cortes and Chagnaud/Yot
Artwork for *Snow White* by Comuicup, Santiago Barreira and Yves Chagnaud
Artwork for *Sleeping Beauty* by Mario Cortes and Yves Chagnaud

Printed in Singapore
First Edition
1 3 5 7 9 10 8 6 4 2
Library of Congress Catalog Card Number on file.

ISBN 0-7868-3715-2

For more Disney Press fun, visit www.disneybooks.com

CONTENTS

Cinderella

Snow White and the Seven Dwarfs

Sleeping Beauty

Cinderella

ONCE UPON A TIME, IN A FARAWAY LAND, THERE WAS A TINY KINGDOM, PEACEFUL AND RICH IN ROMANCE AND TRADITION.

HERE, IN A STATELY HOUSE, THERE LIVED A WIDOWED GENTLEMAN AND HIS LITTLE DAUGHTER, CINDERELLA.

HE WAS A LOVING FATHER, BUT HE DECIDED SHE NEEDED A MOTHER.

AND SO, HE MARRIED A WIDOW WITH TWO DAUGHTERS JUST CINDERELLA'S AGE—ANASTASIA AND DRIZELLA.

CINDERELLA'S FATHER DIED SOON AFTER, AND HER NEW STEPMOTHER WAS REVEALED TO BE A COLD, CRUEL, AND JEALOUS WOMAN.

SHE HATED AND FEARED CINDERELLA'S CHARM AND BEAUTY. SO, SHE TREATED HER OWN DAUGHTERS LIKE PRINCESSES AND CINDERELLA TERRIBLY. EVENTUALLY, CINDERELLA WAS FORCED TO BECOME A SERVANT IN HER OWN HOUSE.

AND YET, THROUGH IT ALL, CINDERELLA REMAINED EVER-GENTLE AND KIND, SO THAT EVEN THE ANIMALS LOVED HER, BECOMING HER ONLY FRIENDS.

FOR WITH EACH NEW DAY, CINDERELLA FOUND NEW HOPE THAT HER DREAMS OF HAPPINESS MIGHT SOMEDAY COME TRUE.

MMM. . . GOOD MORNING! YES, I KNOW IT'S A BEAUTIFUL DAY . . .

. . . BUT IT WAS SUCH A BEAUTIFUL DREAM, TOO.

AND YOU KNOW A DREAM IS JUST A WISH YOUR HEART MAKES.

BING-BONG!

OH, AND THERE'S THE CLOCK! EVEN THAT BOSSES ME AROUND!

AND EVEN WITH A DAY FULL OF HARD WORK AHEAD OF HER, CINDERELLA STARTED HER DAY WITH A SMILE AND A LAUGH.

CINDERELLY! CINDERELLY!

NEW MOUSE! NEBBA SEEN AFORE!

OH, A VISITOR! HOW NICE! WELL, WE'LL HAVE TO WELCOME HIM PROPERLY—AND GET HIM SOME CLOTHES, I'M SURE.

YOU'LL NEED A NAME, WON'T YOU? HOW ABOUT . . . GUS? JAQ, WOULD YOU SHOW GUS THE HOUSE WHILE I GET TO WORK?

"OH, AND JAQ. . ." CINDERELLA CONTINUED, "MAKE SURE GUS KNOWS ALL ABOUT LUCIFER."

LUCIFER—OF ALL THE TERRIBLE THINGS IN CINDERELLA'S LIFE, LUCIFER THE CAT WAS WAY UP ON THE LIST.

LUCIFER! COME!

I KNOW IT'S EARLY—TRUST ME, I KNOW.

BUT THIS IS WHEN I'VE BEEN TOLD TO FEED YOU. AND I DO WHAT I'M TOLD. SO, COME ON.

ZZZ... ZZZ... SNUFF... ZZZ...

DOWN IN THE KITCHEN WAS THE WORLD'S SLEEPIEST DOG. CINDERELLA'S FATHER HAD GIVEN BRUNO TO HIS DAUGHTER. NOW BRUNO WAS OUT OF FAVOR, TOO.

LIKE ALL THE ANIMALS—EXCEPT FOR LUCIFER, OF COURSE—HE WAS COMPLETELY DEVOTED TO CINDERELLA. WHEN HE COULD STAY AWAKE, THAT IS.

RISE AND SHINE, BRUNO! TODAY'S THE DAY YOU TWO FINALLY BECOME FRIENDS.

AFTER ALL, YOU'RE VERY SWEET, BRUNO. AND LUCIFER HAS HIS GOOD POINTS...

...EVEN IF I CAN'T ACTUALLY THINK OF ANY RIGHT NOW.

PERHAPS THAT WAS BECAUSE, FOR ONCE, CINDERELLA WAS MISTAKEN—THERE REALLY WAS NOTHING GOOD ABOUT LUCIFER.

GRRRR!!!

MEOW!

BRUNO! OKAY. . . OUT YOU GO. YOU'LL HAVE BREAKFAST OUTSIDE TODAY.

I KNOW IT ISN'T EASY. . . BELIEVE ME.

BUT WE HAVE TO AT LEAST TRY.

AND THAT GOES FOR YOU, TOO, YOUR MAJESTY.

BRUNO WOULD DO ANYTHING FOR CINDERELLA—EVEN TRY TO BE NICE TO LUCIFER. BUT IT WOULDN'T BE EASY.

...BUT NOTHING COULD KEEP CINDERELLA'S SPIRITS DOWN FOR LONG.

BREAKFAST TIME—THE BEST PART OF THE DAY FOR MOST OF THE ANIMALS. BUT FOR THE MICE, IT MEANT SOMEONE WOULD HAVE TO DISTRACT LUCIFER SO THE OTHERS COULD GATHER FOOD. JAQ WAS THE PERFECT CANDIDATE.

JAQ DID AN OUTSTANDING JOB.

JAQ WAVED THE "ALL CLEAR" SIGN.

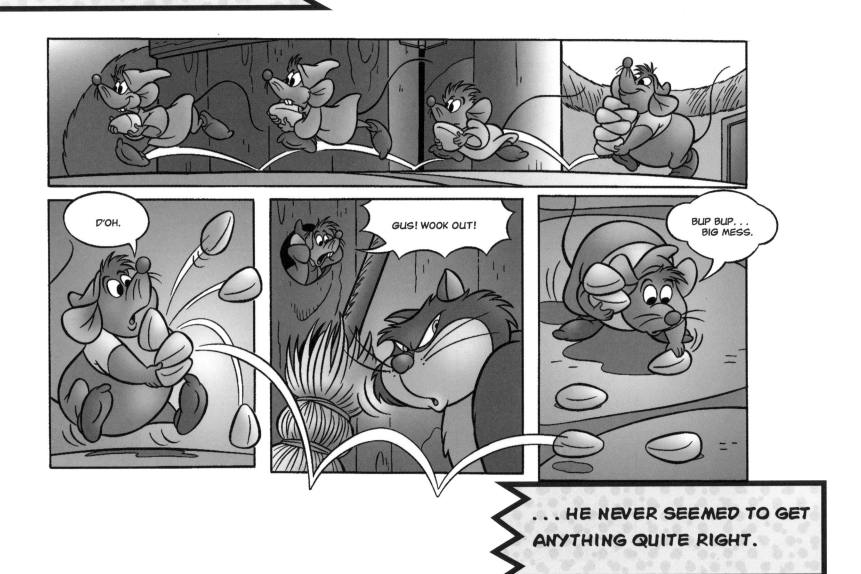

OH, NO, YOU DON'T!

OR MAYBE YOU DO.

NO! DEFINITELY NOT!

HEY. A CLEAN SWEEP.

MEANWHILE, CINDERELLA WENT ON WITH THE NEXT UNPLEASANT TASK OF THE DAY... WITH A GOOD HEART, AS ALWAYS.

SIGH. ALL I DO IS WORK.

WELL! IT'S ABOUT TIME!

WE ALMOST STARVED!

UNFORTUNATELY, GOOD HEART OR NO, CINDERELLA COULDN'T KNOW THAT INSIDE ONE OF THE TEACUPS...

CINDERELLA!

YES, STEPMOTHER?

COME HERE. NOW.

SO . . . IT SEEMS WE HAVE TIME FOR JOKES. PERHAPS I CAN FIND MORE FOR YOU TO DO. TODAY, YOU SHALL CLEAN THE LARGE CARPET IN THE MAIN HALL, WASH ALL THE WINDOWS, AS WELL AS THE TAPESTRIES AND DRAPERIES . . .

. . . AND GIVE LUCIFER A BATH.

MEANWHILE, ELSEWHERE IN THE KINGDOM...

MY SON HAS BEEN AVOIDING THIS LONG ENOUGH! IT'S TIME HE GOT MARRIED AND SETTLED DOWN!

YOUR MAJESTY, WE MUST BE PATIENT.

BUT I'M NOT GETTING ANY YOUNGER. I WANT GRANDCHILDREN.

SO, WE MUST MAKE SURE THE PRINCE MEETS THE RIGHT GIRL UNDER THE RIGHT CONDITIONS.

"IT'S JUST THAT SIMPLE."

SOON, MESSENGERS WERE BEING SENT TO EVERY HOUSEHOLD ACROSS THE LAND.

AN URGENT MESSAGE FROM HIS MAJESTY!

OOH, FROM THE KING! I WONDER WHAT'S SO IMPORTANT!

THE MICE WEREN'T THE ONLY ONES WHO WERE CURIOUS. EVEN CINDERELLA WAS WONDERING.

WELL? WHAT IS IT? YOU CAN'T BE FINISHED WITH THE CLEANING ALREADY!

I'VE A MESSAGE FROM THE PALACE.

THE KING?

GIVE IT HERE!

WELL . . . THERE'S TO BE A BALL IN HONOR OF THE PRINCE. EVERY ELIGIBLE MAIDEN IS TO ATTEND.

WHY, THAT'S US! I'M SO ELIGIBLE!

THAT MEANS I CAN GO, TOO!

HA! YOU, DANCING WITH THE PRINCE?!

"WOULD YA HOLD MY BROOM, YA HIGHNESS?"

IT SAYS, "BY ROYAL COMMAND, EVERY ELIGIBLE MAIDEN IS TO ATTEND."

POOR CINDERELLA. SO GOOD AND LOYAL AND TRUSTING.

EVEN AFTER ALL THIS TIME, SHE HAD NO IDEA HOW WICKED HER STEPMOTHER AND STEPSISTERS COULD BE.

OH, I'VE ALWAYS LOVED THIS DRESS OF MY MOTHER'S.

IT'S A LITTLE OLD-FASHIONED, BUT... LET'S SEE...

OH! THIS IDEA IS PERFECT!

OOH...

DAT'S BOOTEEFUL!

THE ALTERATIONS WILL TAKE A WHILE, BUT I SHOULD BE ABLE TO FINISH JUST IN TIME.

CINDERELLA!

OH, WHAT DO THEY WANT NOW?

OH, WELL... GUESS MY DRESS'LL JUST HAVE TO WAIT.

THEY'RE NEVER GOING TO GIVE HER TIME TO FINISH HER DRESS!

POOR CINDERELLY. SHE'S NOT GOING TO THAT BALL.

BUT... BUT...

BUT... BUT...

"WELL... WHAT IF WE FINISH THE DRESS FOR HER?"

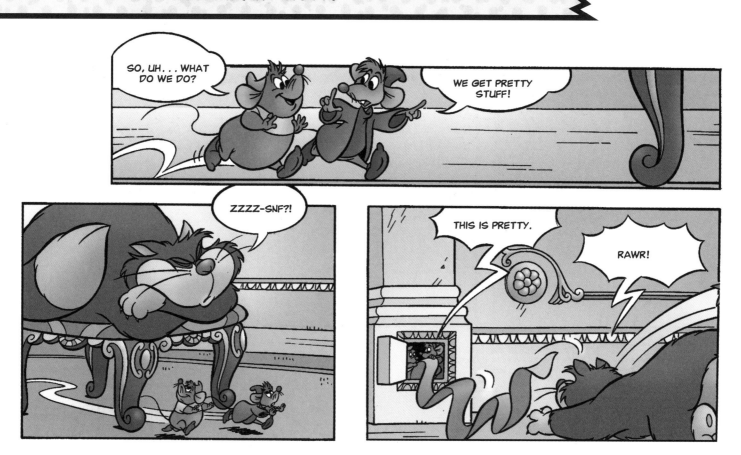

UNFORTUNATELY, STEALING IS NEVER A GOOD IDEA, NO MATTER HOW MUCH THEIR OWNERS MAY HATE THE THINGS OR HOW PURE YOUR INTENTIONS...

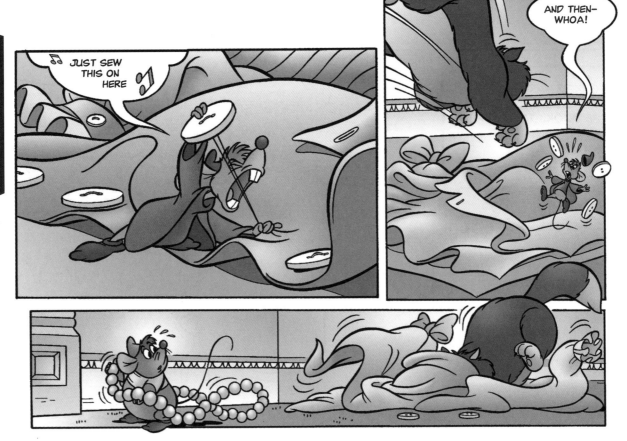

THE ANIMALS WORKED HARD TO MAKE THE DRESS AS BEAUTIFUL AS IT WAS IN THE BOOK, JUST AS CINDERELLA HAD IMAGINED IT— ALMOST AS BEAUTIFUL AS CINDERELLA HERSELF.

AND THEN, ALL TOO SOON, THE NIGHT ARRIVED.

THE CARRIAGE IS HERE.

WHY, YOU'RE NOT READY, CHILD.

I'M NOT GOING.

WHAT A SHAME. THERE WILL BE OTHER TIMES... PERHAPS.

CINDERELLA THOUGHT HER HEART WOULD BREAK.

SHE'D NEVER FELT SO ALONE.

OH, WELL... WHAT'S A ROYAL BALL? I SUPPOSE IT WOULD BE FRIGHTFULLY BORING... AND COMPLETELY WONDERFUL...

OH! WHAT'S...

OH, MY.

SURPRISE!

HAPPY BIRTHDAY!

OH, BOY.

WHY. . . I NEVER DREAMED. . . OH, HOW CAN I EVER THANK YOU?

REMEMBER, WHEN YOU'RE PRESENTED TO THE PRINCE—

PLEASE, WAIT!

CINDERELLA'S STEPMOTHER AND STEPSISTERS COULDN'T BELIEVE THEIR EARS.

DO YOU LIKE MY DRESS?

CINDERELLA?!

ANASTASIA AND DRIZELLA THOUGHT IT WAS THE LOVELIEST DRESS THEY'D EVER SEEN.

SO THEY HATED IT ON CINDERELLA.

MOTHER, YOU CAN'T LET HER COME, YOU JUST CAN'T, SHE'LL RUIN—

GIRLS. PLEASE. AFTER ALL, WE DID MAKE A BARGAIN. DIDN'T WE?

AND I NEVER GO BACK ON MY WORD. DO I?

MY WORD. . . THESE BEADS ARE JUST THE RIGHT TOUCH. . . AREN'T THEY. . . DRIZELLA?

AND WITHOUT ANOTHER WORD, THEY WERE GONE.

OH . . . OH, NO . . . I ALWAYS THOUGHT . . .

. . . BUT NOW . . . THERE'S JUST NOTHING LEFT TO BELIEVE IN.

NOTHING, DEAR? OH, NOW.

SHE FOUND HERSELF OUT IN THE ABANDONED GARDEN WHERE SHE'D PLAYED SO OFTEN WITH HER FATHER WHEN SHE WAS A LITTLE GIRL. NO ONE HAD BEEN THERE SINCE HE HAD DIED.

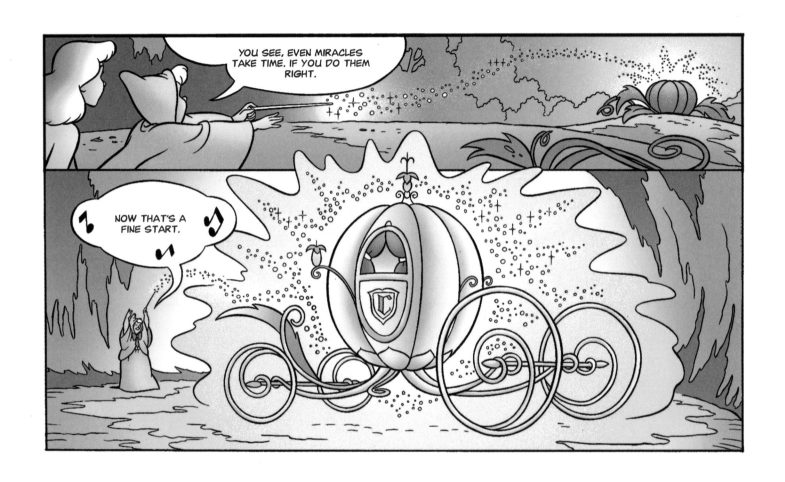

CINDERELLA COULDN'T BELIEVE SHE'D JUST SEEN A PUMPKIN
TURNED INTO A MAGNIFICENT COACH.

NOW, AN ELEGANT COACH LIKE THAT NEEDS . . . MICE!

MICE?

WITH A SMALL CHANGE.

MICE.

NOW, WE NEED A COACHMAN.

AND A FOOTMAN.

DO . . . DO YOU THINK PERHAPS MY DRESS . . . ?

NO! THAT WILL NEVER DO.

BUT A LITTLE NIP HERE AND A TUCK THERE . . .

NOW LISTEN WELL, CHILD. ALL THIS WILL ONLY LAST UNTIL MIDNIGHT. MIDNIGHT, DO YOU HEAR?

"AT THE STROKE OF TWELVE, IT WILL ALL CHANGE BACK. EVERY BIT OF IT," THE FAIRY GODMOTHER SAID.

I CAN'T UNDERSTAND! MY SON HAS SEEN EVERY SINGLE MAIDEN IN THE KINGDOM! HASN'T HE?

THEY'RE ALL HERE, SIRE. HE DOESN'T LIKE—

THE MADEMOISELLES DRIZELLA AND ANASTASIA TREMAINE!

HMM? WHAT'S ALL THIS THEN?

WHO . . . IS . . . *THAT*?!

IT SEEMS, SIRE, THAT THAT IS WHAT YOUR SON, THE PRINCE, WOULD ALSO CARE TO KNOW.

44

WHO IS SHE? CAN YOU SEE?

I CAN'T SEE A THING!

I DON'T BELIEVE I'VE EVER SEEN HER BEFORE... AND YET...

THE PRINCE LED CINDERELLA TO HIS FAVORITE SPOTS, WHERE THEY TALKED FOR HOURS.

AND ALL TOO SOON . . .

OH! IT'S MIDNIGHT!

I MUST GO!

BUT . . . NO, PLEASE WAIT!

I'M SO SORRY!

BUT . . . BUT I DON'T EVEN KNOW YOUR NAME!

THE DUKE HAD BEEN MAKING SURE THE YOUNG COUPLE WASN'T DISTURBED. HE WAS STUNNED WHEN CINDERELLA SUDDENLY RAN PAST.

AND JUST AS THE CLOCK FINALLY STRUCK TWELVE...

...EVERYTHING CHANGED BACK TO THE WAY IT WAS.

OH, WASN'T THAT ALL JUST SO LOVELY. I MET THE NICEST MAN. I'M SURE EVEN THE PRINCE HIMSELF COULDN'T HAVE BEEN MORE WONDERFUL.

CINDERELLY! YOUR SLIPPER! IT DIDN'T CHANGE!

OH . . . OH, THANK YOU, FAIRY GODMOTHER.

"THANK YOU FOR THE MOST WONDERFUL EVENING EVER."

GIRLS! LISTEN! THE GRAND DUKE HAS BEEN HUNTING ALL NIGHT FOR THE GIRL WHO LOST HER GLASS SLIPPER AT THE BALL LAST NIGHT. THEY SAY THE PRINCE IS MADLY IN LOVE WITH HER!

SOON THE NEWS SPREAD TO EVERY CORNER OF THE KINGDOM.

CRASH! DING-BLING!

THE . . . THE PRINCE? THAT WAS THE PRINCE?

YOU CLUMSY OX! CLEAN THAT UP!

CLEAN UP? OH, YES . . . YES . . . I MUST CLEAN UP.

. . . AND I SHOULD CHANGE THIS DRESS, TOO . . .

MOTHER . . . YOU DON'T THINK—

SHE CAN'T BE THE ONE—

QUIET. THE PRINCE DOESN'T KNOW WHO FITS THAT SLIPPER.

AND SO, THE STEPMOTHER CLIMBED THE STAIRS TO CINDERELLA'S ROOM.

HE WAS SO SWEET . . . AND A PRINCE!

HMM?

...WHERE CINDERELLA WAS READYING HERSELF, UNAWARE OF HER STEPMOTHER'S SCHEME.

OH, NO!

NO! PLEASE! UNLOCK THE DOOR! I MUST SEE HIM AGAIN!

ANNOUNCING THE GRAND DUKE!

THANK YOU. YOU HONOR OUR HUMBLE HOME.

YES. QUITE SO.

MAY I PRESENT MY DAUGHTERS, DRIZELLA AND ANASTASIA.

YOUR GRACE.

YES, WELL. "ALL ROYAL SUBJECTS OF HIS IMPERIAL MAJESTY ARE NOTIFIED BY PROCLAMATION THAT THIS GLASS SLIPPER MUST—"

WHY, THAT'S MY SLIPPER!

OH, NO! IT'S MINE!

GIRLS! GIRLS! CONTROL YOURSELVES! REMEMBER YOUR MANNERS. A THOUSAND PARDONS, YOUR GRACE.

HMM. YES. QUITE SO. AS I WAS SAYING. ". . . THIS GLASS SLIPPER MUST–"

"–BE PLACED ONTO THE FOOT OF EVERY SINGLE MAIDEN IN THE KINGDOM–"

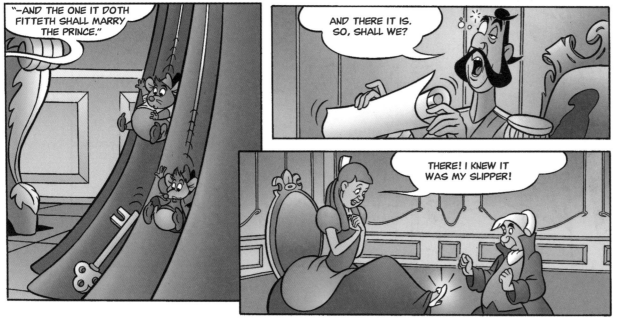

"–AND THE ONE IT DOTH FITTETH SHALL MARRY THE PRINCE."

AND THERE IT IS. SO, SHALL WE?

THERE! I KNEW IT WAS MY SLIPPER!

TO THE SHOCK AND HORROR OF THE DUKE AND HIS FOOTMAN, IT WAS A PERFECT FIT.

ALMOST.

I DON'T UNDERSTAND. IT ALWAYS FIT PERFECTLY BEFORE.

COME ON, GUS! WE GOTTA HURRY AND GET CINDERELLY THE KEY BEFORE IT'S TOO LATE!

OH, BOY.

"THAT'S . . . THAT'S A LOT OF STAIRS."

I DON'T THINK YOU'RE REALLY TRYING TO GET IT TO FIT!

THEY HAD FORGOTTEN ABOUT LUCIFER!

ONCE AGAIN, CINDERELLA FELT LIKE SHE WAS SO CLOSE... AND YET STILL SO FAR...

LUCIFER, PLEASE—LET HIM GO!

ROWR!

!?

THE BIRDS AND MICE WERE TERRIFIED OF LUCIFER. BUT NOTHING WOULD STOP THEM FROM TRYING TO HELP CINDERELLA.

CINDERELLA KNEW SOMEONE ELSE WHO WOULD HELP...IF HE COULD JUST WAKE UP...

QUICK! GET BRUNO! GO GET BRUNO!

WHILE DOWN IN THE MAIN HALL...

URG...ENH... UNH...IT...

IT FITS? IT FITS!

IT FITS!?

NOT REALLY.

OH, MY!

"THAT WAS CLOSE."

TWEET, TWEET!

OH, MY.

BRUNO WOULD HAVE DONE ANYTHING FOR CINDERELLA. IF HE COULD ONLY WAKE UP.

THE HORSE DECIDED
TO HELP.

THAT DID THE TRICK. BRUNO
WAS OFF LIKE A SHOT.

LUCIFER WAS MIGHTY BRAVE WHEN IT CAME TO
CATS AND MICE. WITH AN ANGRY DOG, THOUGH . . .
NOT SO MUCH.

YOU ARE THE ONLY LADIES OF THE HOUSE, I HOPE? I MEAN, I PRESUME?

THERE'S NO ONE ELSE.

QUITE SO. GOOD DAY, THEN, MADAM. AND I—

WAIT!

PLEASE, MAY I TRY ON THE SLIPPER?

THE DUKE WAS NO FOOL. ONE LOOK AT CINDERELLA
... AND HE KNEW. *THIS GIRL WAS DIFFERENT.*

BRING ME HER—THE—THE SLIPPER.

. . . CINDERELLA'S STEPMOTHER ALWAYS HAD ONE MORE TRICK UP HER SLEEVE.

THE SLIPPER SHATTERED, THERE SEEMED NO WAY TO PROVE CINDERELLA WAS THE GIRL OF THE PRINCE'S DREAMS.

NO! NO, NO, NO, NO, NO!!! WHAT WILL THE KING SAY? WHAT WILL HE DO?

YOUR GRACE? IF IT WILL HELP . . .

"...I HAVE THE OTHER SLIPPER."

OH. OH, MY. OH, YES. QUITE SO.

YAY!!! CINDERELLY!

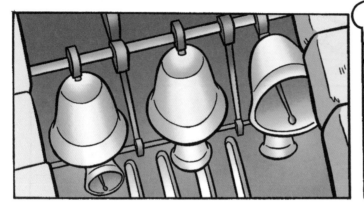

THERE SHE IS!

THANK YOU ALL! I LOVE YOU!

...THAT THE PRINCE AND CINDERELLA WERE SOON MARRIED...

THE END

AND THEY LIVED HAPPILY EVER AFTER.

Snow White

and the Seven Dwarfs

ONCE UPON A TIME, THERE LIVED A LOVELY LITTLE PRINCESS NAMED SNOW WHITE. HER VAIN AND WICKED STEPMOTHER, THE QUEEN, FEARED THAT SOMEDAY SNOW WHITE'S BEAUTY WOULD SURPASS HER OWN. SO, SHE DRESSED THE LITTLE PRINCESS IN RAGS AND FORCED HER TO WORK AS A SCULLERY MAID IN HER OWN CASTLE.

EACH DAY, THE QUEEN CONSULTED HER MAGIC MIRROR.

"MAGIC MIRROR ON THE WALL . . .

" . . . WHO IS THE FAIREST ONE OF ALL?"

YOU ARE, MY QUEEN!

AND AS LONG AS THE MIRROR REPLIED "YOU ARE THE FAIREST ONE OF ALL, MY QUEEN," SNOW WHITE WAS SAFE.

—YOUR WISH JUST MIGHT COME TRUE.

SO . . . I WISH FOR SOMEONE TO LOVE.

I'M WISHING TO HEAR ALL THE NICE THINGS HE'LL SAY.

. . . THINGS HE'LL SAY . . .

TODAY?

THE WISHING WELL WORKED BETTER THAN SNOW WHITE HAD EXPECTED.

IT WAS BAD ENOUGH THAT SNOW WHITE WAS NOW MORE BEAUTIFUL THAN HER STEPMOTHER. BUT FOR HER TO HAVE ALSO FOUND TRUE LOVE . . .

THE HUNTSMAN HAD BEEN THE QUEEN'S MOST TRUSTED SERVANT FOR YEARS. AND HE KNEW WHAT HAPPENED TO THOSE FEW PEOPLE WHO DISOBEYED HER.

SO TO THE FOREST THEY WENT.

OH, ISN'T THIS JUST THE LOVELIEST DAY? I'VE NEVER BEEN OUT THIS FAR BEFORE—THANK YOU SO MUCH FOR BRINGING ME!

HELLO, MY LITTLE FRIENDS—WHAT'S WRONG?

OH!

I . . .

SNOW WHITE RAN AS SHE'D NEVER RUN BEFORE.

SHE'D NEVER BEEN SO FRIGHTENED IN HER LIFE.

NO MATTER WHERE SHE TURNED—

—THERE WAS SOMETHING TERRIFYING. EYES WATCHING HER...

...WATER TO DROWN IN...

...MONSTERS TO EAT HER...

...IT WAS ALL TOO MUCH.

EXHAUSTED...

...SHE FELL.

THEY LED HER EVER DEEPER INTO THE FOREST, THROUGH ITS WONDROUS BEAUTIES...

...UNTIL THEY REACHED...

OH, MY.

IT'S JUST LIKE A DOLLHOUSE!

SEVEN TINY CHAIRS—CHILDREN MUST LIVE HERE! MESSY CHILDREN!

WELL, I CAN FIX THAT.

IF THERE WAS ONE THING SNOW WHITE WAS GOOD AT, IT WAS CLEANING. AND NOW SHE CLEANED AS NEVER BEFORE.

WELL, THAT'S CERTAINLY MUCH BETTER. WON'T THEY BE PLEASED?

NOW, LET'S SEE WHAT'S UPSTAIRS.

OH, WHAT ADORABLE LITTLE BEDS—WITH NAMES ON THEM!

DIGGING WAS ALL THE SEVEN DWARFS REALLY LOVED IN THE WHOLE WORLD. BUT EVEN THEY HAD TO REST, SO OFF TOWARD HOME THEY MARCHED...

...WITH NO IDEA WHAT AWAITED THEM...

... NAMELY ONE SLEEPY LITTLE PRINCESS, TOO TIRED FROM CLEANING TO KEEP HER EYES OPEN.

BUT THE ANIMALS—

—HEARD SOMEONE COMING... AND RAN!

TRYING NOT TO SHOW EACH OTHER HOW SCARED THEY WERE, THE DWARFS MADE THEIR WAY UPSTAIRS...WHERE THEY FOUND...

SHH...

A GIANT!

A MONSTER!

TAKES UP THREE BEDS!

QUICK, BEFORE IT WAKES UP!

TOO LATE!

THE GIANT MONSTER MOVED...

...SAT UP...STRETCHED...AND...

OH!

...WAS REVEALED...

SNOW WHITE COULD SEE THAT GRUMPY WASN'T GOING TO BE EASY TO WIN OVER.

AND WHAT'S YOUR NAME?

OH, OF COURSE. I'M SNOW WHITE.

WHAT?!

THE PRINCESS?

WELL, OF COURSE. NOW YOU BE NICE!

I'LL BE NICE WHEN SHE'S GONE!

OH, PLEASE DON'T SEND ME AWAY. IF YOU DO, MY STEPMOTHER-THE QUEEN-SHE'LL . . .

OH, BOO HOO!

BUT IF YOU LET ME STAY, I'LL CLEAN AND—

WE LIKE DIRT.

AND OF COURSE I'LL COOK.

COOK?! FOOD?!

WHY, OF COURSE! I MADE SOUP FOR DINNER AND—

SHE STAYS!

FEH. GONNA POISON US ALL. YOU'LL SEE.

SNOW WHITE, OF COURSE, WOULD NEVER DO SUCH A THING. HER STEPMOTHER, ON THE OTHER HAND...

I'LL GO TO THE DWARFS' COTTAGE IN DISGUISE. FIRST I'LL NEED MUMMY DUST TO MAKE ME OLD AND THE BLACK OF NIGHT TO SHROUD MY CLOTHES.

AN OLD HAG'S CACKLE TO AGE MY VOICE AND A SCREAM OF FRIGHT TO WHITEN MY HAIR.

YES! NOW BEGIN THY MAGIC SPELL!

THE WICKED QUEEN POURED THE EVIL BREW DOWN HER THROAT...

AAAAAAHHH!!!

BWAH-HA-HA!

CAW!

AH . . .

WHILE HER EVIL STEPMOTHER PLOTTED, SNOW WHITE WAS HAVING THE TIME OF HER LIFE.

SHE'D NEVER HAD SO MUCH FUN BEFORE.

OH! BUT I DON'T KNOW WHERE I'M SLEEPING!

WHY, YOU CAN HAVE OUR ROOM, OF COURSE.

OH, THANK YOU ALL SO MUCH FOR SUCH A WONDERFUL EVENING—I'VE NEVER BEEN HAPPIER. BUT NOW IT'S BEDTIME!

"WE'LL BE JUST FINE DOWN HERE. NONE OF US MIND A BIT."

PERFECT. A PERFECT APPLE . . .

. . . DIPPED IN JUST THE PERFECT POISON. . .

. . . CREATES "THE SLEEPING DEATH!" ONE TASTE AND THE VICTIM'S EYES CLOSE FOREVER!

BUT WAIT! AM I FORGETTING SOMETHING?

QUICKLY, THE WICKED QUEEN FLIPPED THROUGH HER BOOK OF BLACK-MAGIC SPELLS.

NOTHING MUST STOP ME FROM AGAIN BEING FAIREST IN THE LAND!

AHA!

AN ANTIDOTE!

"THE VICTIM CAN BE REVIVED ONLY BY LOVE'S FIRST KISS." WELL, NO FEAR OF THAT.

THE DWARFS WILL THINK HER DEAD. SHE'LL BE BURIED...

...ALIVE.

AT DAWN, THE DWARFS LEFT FOR WORK, AS USUAL. WELL, NOT QUITE AS USUAL. AFTER ALL, THEY DIDN'T NORMALLY HAVE A PRINCESS LIVING WITH THEM.

REMEMBER, NO ONE MUST KNOW YOU'RE HERE! BEWARE OF STRANGERS! LET NO ONE IN!

SNOW WHITE SENT THE DWARFS ON THEIR WAY TO WORK MORE HAPPILY THAN THEY'D EVER GONE BEFORE.

AH... THEY'VE LEFT HER ALONE... AND SHE'LL NEVER SUSPECT...

". . . A HARMLESS OLD WOMAN SELLING APPLES."

OH, MY FRIENDS, THANK YOU FOR BRINGING ME HERE!

WHO'D HAVE THOUGHT HAVING TO RUN AWAY WOULD BE SO WONDERFUL?

IF ONLY I WAS ABLE TO SEE THAT BOY FROM THE WELL AGAIN, I–

BAKING, MY PET?

OH!

MAKING A PIE FOR THE LITTLE MEN, HMM? YES?

SNOW WHITE WAS STARTLED. . . AND FRIGHTENED. . .

YES, A GOOSEBERRY PIE.

GOOSEBERRY?

OH, NO, NO, NO. IT'S APPLE PIES THAT MAKE THE LITTLE MEN'S MOUTHS WATER.

OH, IT DOES LOOK DELICIOUS... BUT...

JUST WAIT UNTIL YOU TASTE ONE, DEARIE. LIKE TO TRY ONE, HMM?

THE DWARFS HAD SAID NOT TO LET ANYONE IN.

THE ANIMALS WEREN'T FOOLED BY THE QUEEN'S MAGIC—
THEY KNEW WHO SHE REALLY WAS . . .

SHAME ON YOU, FRIGHTENING AN OLD LADY!

OH, MY HEART . . . TAKE ME INTO THE HOUSE FOR A DRINK OF WATER.

OF COURSE— I'M SO SORRY.

OH, YOU'VE BEEN SO GOOD . . . SO I'LL SHARE A SECRET WITH YOU.

THIS IS NO ORDINARY APPLE.

DESPERATE TO SAVE SNOW WHITE, THE ANIMALS WENT TO THE MINE. THERE, THEY TRIED EVERYTHING THEY COULD THINK OF TO GET THE DWARFS TO COME HOME RIGHT AWAY.

. . . AM THE FAIREST IN THE LAND AGAIN!

HEE!

NOW, BACK TO MY CASTLE TO BECOME BEAUTIFUL AGAIN!

I'LL . . . HMM? WHAT'S THAT?

THE WICKED STEPMOTHER MAY HAVE LOOKED OLD, BUT THERE WAS NOTHING WRONG WITH HER EARS.

BUT UNLIKE THE DWARFS, SHE'D NEVER BEEN TO THIS PART OF THE FOREST BEFORE.

DON'T LET HER GET AWAY!

COME ON—AFTER HER!

THEY'RE TOO FAST!

I'M GOING TO BE TRAPPED!

THE QUEEN THOUGHT SHE'D SUDDENLY COME UP WITH THE PERFECT PLAN.

ROLL THE BOULDER ONTO THE DWARFS, AND ALL HER PROBLEMS WOULD DISAPPEAR.

A-HA-HA-HA-HA!

BUT SO WICKED WAS SNOW WHITE'S STEPMOTHER . . .

. . . THAT EVEN NATURE ITSELF DESPISED HER. A BOLT OF LIGHTNING SHATTERED HER STAFF AND THREW HER OVER THE EDGE OF THE CLIFF.

WHEN THE DWARFS RETURNED HOME, THEIR WORST FEARS WERE REALIZED.

WE WERE TOO LATE! SHE'S GONE.

HEARTBROKEN, THEY BUILT A GLASS COFFIN . . .

. . . UNABLE TO FACE THE IDEA OF SAYING GOOD-BYE TO THEIR BELOVED SNOW WHITE FOREVER. THEY STAYED BY HER SIDE DAY AND NIGHT FOR WEEKS.

TALES SPREAD FAR AND WIDE OF THE BEAUTIFUL PRINCESS LOCKED IN ETERNAL SLEEP.

ONE DAY, THE NEWS EVEN REACHED THE EARS OF A CERTAIN PRINCE, WHO WONDERED IF THIS COULD BE THE GIRL OF HIS DREAMS. HE'D ONLY SEEN HER ONCE, BUT HE'D SEARCHED FOR HER EVERY DAY SINCE. ONE LOOK AT SNOW WHITE, AND HE KNEW HE'D FOUND HER AGAIN... ONLY TO SAY GOOD-BYE ONE LAST TIME.

. . . FOR THE FIRST KISS OF TRUE LOVE.

HOORAY!!!

WELL NOW! WE DIDN'T SEE *THAT* COMING!

OH . . . THANK YOU ALL SO MUCH FOR EVERYTHING.

I'LL MISS YOU SO MUCH—BUT I'LL COME BACK. I PROMISE.

AND DON'T FORGET TO CLEAN UP . . . ONCE IN A WHILE!

GOOD-BYE! GOOD-BYE!

Sleeping Beauty

ONCE UPON A TIME, IN A FARAWAY LAND, LIVED A KING AND HIS FAIR QUEEN. FOR MANY YEARS KING STEFAN AND QUEEN LEAH LONGED FOR A CHILD AND, AT LONG LAST, THEIR WISH WAS GRANTED.

A DAUGHTER WAS BORN.

THEY NAMED HER AURORA, AFTER THE DAWN, FOR SHE FILLED THEIR LIVES WITH SUNSHINE.

A GREAT HOLIDAY WAS PROCLAIMED THROUGHOUT THE KINGDOM, SO ALL MIGHT PAY HOMAGE TO THE BELOVED INFANT PRINCESS.

THIS WAS THE YOUNG PRINCE'S FIRST LOOK AT HIS BRIDE-TO-BE.

EVEN KING HUBERT AND PRINCE PHILLIP CAME. THE TWO KINGS HAD ALREADY ARRANGED FOR PHILLIP AND AURORA TO BE MARRIED WHEN THEY WERE OLD ENOUGH.

AND THEN THE *OTHER* GUESTS-OF-HONOR MADE THEIR ENTRANCES.

THE THREE GOOD FAIRIES—MISTRESSES FLORA, FAUNA, AND MERRYWEATHER!

WE ARE HONORED!

THE LITTLE DARLING!

YOUR MAJESTIES, WE'D LIKE TO GIVE THE PRINCESS OUR GIFTS NOW.

I SHALL GIVE HER THE GIFT OF BEAUTY.

I SHALL GIVE THE GIFT OF SONG.

BUT BEFORE MERRYWEATHER COULD GIVE HER GIFT—

THE KING AND QUEEN WERE DISTRAUGHT, BUT THE FAIRIES TRIED TO LOOK ON THE BRIGHT SIDE.

DON'T DESPAIR, YOUR MAJESTIES—MERRYWEATHER STILL HAS HER GIFT TO GIVE.

THEN SHE CAN UNDO THIS FEARFUL CURSE?

WELL... NO. MALEFICENT'S POWERS ARE FAR TOO GREAT. BUT SHE CAN HELP.

OH, DEAR. PRINCESS, IF YOUR FINGER SHOULD PRICK A SPINNING WHEEL'S SPINDLE, YOU'LL NOT DIE...

...BUT MERELY SLEEP, UNTIL TRUE LOVE'S FIRST KISS SHOULD AWAKEN YOU.

BUT KING STEFAN, STILL FEARFUL FOR HIS DAUGHTER'S LIFE, DID DECREE THAT EVERY SPINNING WHEEL IN THE KINGDOM BE BURNED. THE FIRE LIT THE NIGHT SKY FOR MILES.

THE KING WAS DOING HIS BEST FOR HIS DAUGHTER. BUT THE FAIRIES KNEW IT WOULD NEVER BE ENOUGH TO STOP MALEFICENT.

THE KING AND QUEEN WERE HEARTBROKEN AT THE THOUGHT OF SAYING GOOD-BYE TO THEIR LITTLE GIRL. BUT THEY KNEW IT WAS FOR THE BEST.

AND SO THE FAIRIES, DISGUISED AS HUMANS, SNUCK OFF IN THE MIDDLE OF THE NIGHT WITH PRINCESS AURORA.

AND THAT WAS THE LAST ANYONE SAW OR HEARD OF THEM FOR ALMOST SIXTEEN YEARS.

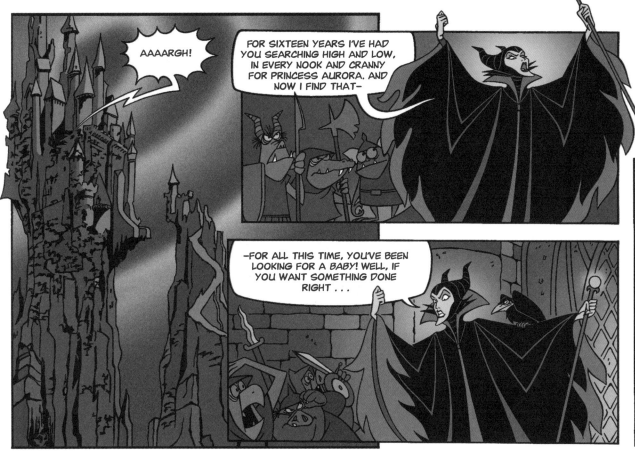

AAAARGH!

FOR SIXTEEN YEARS I'VE HAD
YOU SEARCHING HIGH AND LOW,
IN EVERY NOOK AND CRANNY
FOR PRINCESS AURORA. AND
NOW I FIND THAT—

—FOR ALL THIS TIME, YOU'VE BEEN
LOOKING FOR A BABY! WELL, IF
YOU WANT SOMETHING DONE
RIGHT . . .

MY PET, YOU ARE MY LAST
HOPE. CIRCLE FAR AND WIDE.
SEARCH FOR A MAID OF SIXTEEN
WITH HAIR OF SUNSHINE GOLD
AND LIPS RED AS THE ROSE.

MALEFICENT KNEW TIME WAS SHORT—IT WAS ALMOST PRINCESS AURORA'S SIXTEENTH BIRTHDAY. AND IN ALL THAT TIME, NO ONE HAD EVER VENTURED DEEP, DEEP INTO THE FOREST, WHERE THREE PEASANTS HAD RAISED A LITTLE GIRL THEY CALLED BRIAR ROSE.

THE THREE HAPPY WOMEN WERE, EVEN NOW, STILL TRYING TO LEARN HOW TO MAKE A DRESS AND BAKE A CAKE.

WHAT ARE YOU UP TO?

ROSE! WHO, US? UP TO SOMETHING?

BERRIES! WE NEED BERRIES!

BUT I PICKED BERRIES YESTERDAY.

OH, WE NEED LOTS MORE.

SO TAKE YOUR TIME.

THE FAIRIES QUICKLY HUSTLED THE YOUNG PRINCESS OUT THE DOOR.

SHE KNEW THEY WERE UP TO SOMETHING, BUT SHE WAS PERFECTLY HAPPY TO PLAY ALONG.

DON'T HURRY BACK!

BUT DON'T GO TOO FAR, DEAR! AND DON'T TALK TO ANY STRANGERS!

DO YOU THINK SHE SUSPECTS?

OF COURSE NOT. OH, WILL SHE BE SURPRISED WITH HER NEW DRESS!

AND A REAL CAKE!

I'LL GET THE WANDS!

BUT THE FAIRIES HADN'T USED MAGIC YET, AND THEY WERE A BIT AFRAID TO START ON THEIR LAST DAY IN THE WOODS. SO THEY DECIDED TO WORK *WITHOUT* MAGIC.

WONDERING AND WANDERING, THE YOUNG PRINCESS BEGAN TO SING, AS SHE ALWAYS DID.

I WONDER WHY EACH LITTLE BIRD HAS SOMEONE TO SING TO, YET I'M ALL ALONE. WILL I EVER FIND TRUE LOVE?

THE PRINCE HAD NEVER BEEN THIS DEEP IN THE FOREST BEFORE, AND HE WAS SURPRISED TO FIND SOMEONE ELSE SO FAR FROM CIVILIZATION—

—AND WITH THE MOST BEAUTIFUL VOICE HE'D EVER HEARD.

WHOA! WHAT IS THAT BEAUTIFUL SOUND? CAN. . . CAN THAT BE SOMEONE SINGING? WAY OUT HERE?

DEAR AUNT FLORA AND AUNT FAUNA AND AUNT MERRYWEATHER.

THEY NEVER WANT ME TO MEET ANYONE.

THEY TREAT ME LIKE A CHILD. BUT I DID MEET SOMEONE! A PRINCE!

"OF COURSE, IT WAS ONLY IN MY DREAM. BUT THEY SAY IF YOU DREAM SOMETHING MORE THAN ONCE..." AURORA BEGAN.

"... IT'S SURE TO COME TRUE."

I KNOW I HEARD SOMEONE SINGING. SHE MUST BE AROUND... SOMEWHERE?

STOP!

HEY!

AURORA KNEW HER ANIMAL FRIENDS WERE TRYING TO CHEER HER UP.

SHE DECIDED TO LET THEM.

OH, MY. HOW DO YOU DO?

DANCE? I'D LOVE TO.

AFTER ALL, WE HAVE MET—OH!

IN A DREAM?

I'M SORRY—I DIDN'T MEAN TO FRIGHTEN YOU.

AND AURORA FLED BACK TO THAT COTTAGE . . .

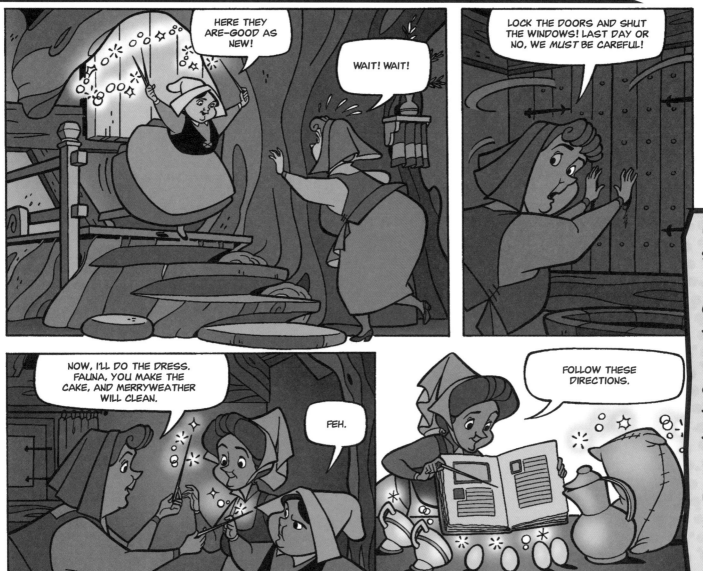

HERE THEY ARE—GOOD AS NEW!

WAIT! WAIT!

LOCK THE DOORS AND SHUT THE WINDOWS! LAST DAY OR NO, WE MUST BE CAREFUL!

NOW, I'LL DO THE DRESS. FAUNA, YOU MAKE THE CAKE, AND MERRYWEATHER WILL CLEAN.

FEH.

FOLLOW THESE DIRECTIONS.

EVEN AFTER SIXTEEN LONG YEARS OF DOING THE COOKING AND THE CLEANING THEMSELVES, THE GOOD FAIRIES HADN'T FORGOTTEN A BIT OF MAGIC.

154

NOR HAD THEY LEARNED HOW TO AGREE.

OH, IT'S LOVELY. BUT MAKE IT BLUE.

NOT A CHANCE. MAKE IT PINK.

THE TWO FAIRIES HAD ARGUED OVER WHICH WAS THE PRETTIEST COLOR FOR CENTURIES, AND THEY WEREN'T ABOUT TO STOP NOW THAT IT CAME TO AURORA'S SPECIAL DRESS.

ARK?

BUT FLYING HIGH OVER THE FOREST, MALEFICENT'S PET CROW NOTICED THE TELLTALE SIGNS OF MAGIC FAR BELOW.

IN THE COTTAGE, THE GOOD FAIRIES HEARD THEIR PRECIOUS PRINCESS COMING HOME.

HMM?

QUICK, HIDE!

AS IF HER DAY HADN'T ALREADY BEEN UNUSUAL ENOUGH—MEETING A PERSON OTHER THAN HER "AUNTS" FOR THE FIRST TIME EVER—AURORA WAS SHOCKED TO DISCOVER THE MOST BEAUTIFUL DRESS SHE COULD POSSIBLY IMAGINE, AND, AN INCREDIBLE CAKE!

FOR SIXTEEN LONG YEARS, THE GOOD FAIRIES HAD WASHED AND FED AND CLOTHED AND TAUGHT THEIR PRINCESS, WAITING FOR THE DAY THEY COULD TELL HER THE TRUTH.

BUT AURORA WANTED TO BE WITH THE STRANGER SHE MET IN THE WOODS.

OH, NO. . . NO!

AND WE ALWAYS THOUGHT SHE'D BE SO HAPPY.

BUT AURORA AND THE GOOD FAIRIES WEREN'T THE ONLY ONES TO BE SURPRISED THAT DAY.

AS THE DARK OF NIGHT BEGAN TO FALL, THE GOOD FAIRIES SNUCK PRINCESS AURORA, AT LONG LAST, BACK INTO HER CASTLE HOME.

HERE YOU ARE, DEAR, HOME AGAIN AT LAST. I KNOW YOU'VE BEEN THROUGH SO MUCH TODAY, BUT IT'S ALMOST OVER.

FAUNA AND MERRYWEATHER LOCKED THE DOORS AND CLOSED THE CURTAINS SO NO ONE COULD KNOW OF THE PRINCESS'S PRESENCE.

OH, BUT ONE FINAL GIFT, FIRST— SOMETHING A TRUE PRINCESS NEEDS.

THERE.

OH, DEAR. . . PERHAPS A FEW MINUTES ALONE.

IT'S THAT BOY— WHAT WILL WE DO?

INSIDE THE ROOM, THE DISMAYED PRINCESS SOON FOUND THERE WAS SOMETHING ELSE SHE COULDN'T FIGHT...

... A SPELL CAST OVER HER BY MALEFICENT.

PRINCESS AURORA WAS UNDER A SPELL, COMPLETELY UNAWARE OF WHAT SHE WAS DOING. MALEFICENT TRANSFORMED HERSELF INTO A SPINNING WHEEL, AND MADE AURORA PRICK HER FINGER.

THE GOOD FAIRIES SENSED SHE WAS IN TROUBLE AND RUSHED IN . . .

. . . BUT THEY WERE TOO LATE.

YOU FOOLS THOUGHT YOU COULD DEFEAT ME.

WELL, HERE'S YOUR PRECIOUS PRINCESS.

ROSE!

OH, I'LL NEVER FORGIVE MYSELF.

WE'RE ALL TO BLAME.

UNAWARE OF THE TRUE IDENTITY OF HIS BELOVED, PRINCE PHILLIP ARRIVED AT THE COTTAGE, JUST AS REQUESTED.

COME IN.

THE MOMENT THE DOOR SLAMMED BEHIND HIM, HE HAD A FEELING SOMETHING MIGHT BE WRONG.

OH, NO! THE PRINCE'S HAT! WE'RE TOO LATE!

AGAIN!

MALEFICENT MUST HAVE TAKEN HIM TO THE FORBIDDEN MOUNTAIN.

WE. . . WE CAN'T GO THERE! CAN WE?

WE CAN.

"AND WE WILL!"

WHAT A PITY PRINCE PHILLIP CAN'T BE HERE TO ENJOY THE CELEBRATION. WE MUST GO TO THE DUNGEON TO CHEER HIM UP.

WHY SO SAD, PRINCE PHILLIP? A WONDROUS FUTURE LIES BEFORE YOU—THE DESTINED HERO OF A CHARMING FAIRY TALE COME TRUE.

BEHOLD! KING STEPHAN'S CASTLE, AND IN THE TOPMOST TOWER, DREAMING OF HER TRUE LOVE...

... THE PRINCESS AURORA—THE VERY SAME PEASANT MAID WHO WON THE HEART OF OUR NOBLE PRINCE BUT YESTERDAY.

"... FOR THE FIRST TIME IN SIXTEEN YEARS."

THE VERY MOMENT MALEFICENT WAS GONE...

SHH. NOT A SOUND.

THE ROAD TO TRUE LOVE MAY HAVE STILL MORE DANGERS FOR YOU TO FACE.

AND SO—AN ENCHANTED SHIELD OF VIRTUE.

AND A MIGHTY SWORD OF TRUTH.

CAW!

CAW!

LIKE A SHOT, THE PRINCE WAS OFF TO SAVE HIS TRUE LOVE.

SOON THE ENTIRE PLACE WAS IN AN UPROAR. MALEFICENT WAS NOT HAPPY TO BE AWAKENED. SHE WAS EVEN LESS HAPPY WHEN SHE FOUND OUT WHY.

NO ONE REFUSES MY HOSPITALITY!

SHE SENT OUT A MIGHTY BURST—

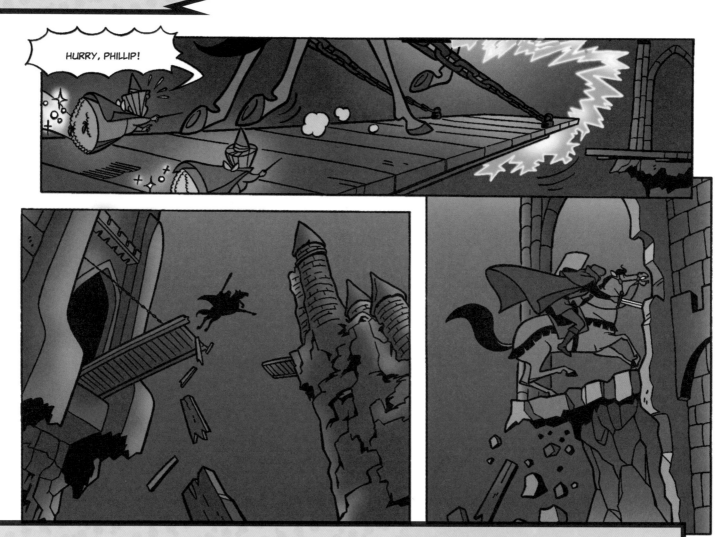

HURRY, PHILLIP!

—BUT TO NO AVAIL. THIS TRUE-LOVE THING SHE'D MOCKED WAS TURNING OUT TO BE TOUGHER THAN SHE'D EXPECTED.

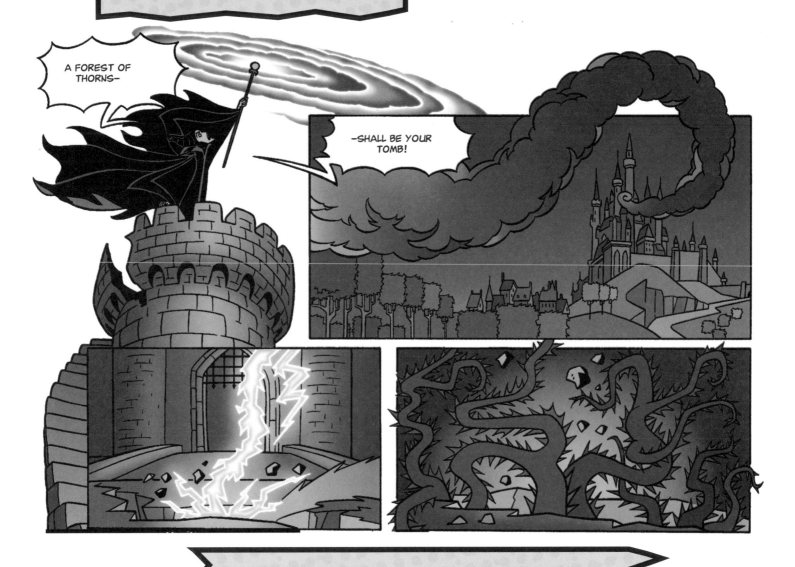

—ERUPTED A FOREST OF THORNS. NO ONE AND NOTHING COULD GET THROUGH.

CHARGE!

EXCEPT TRUE LOVE.

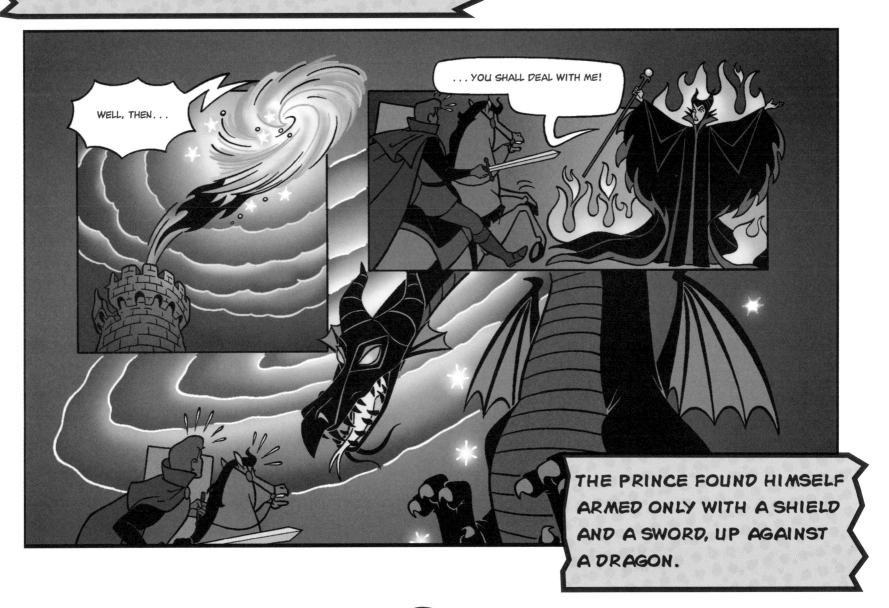

MALEFICENT DECIDED TO TAKE MATTERS INTO HER OWN HANDS.

THE PRINCE FOUND HIMSELF ARMED ONLY WITH A SHIELD AND A SWORD, UP AGAINST A DRAGON.

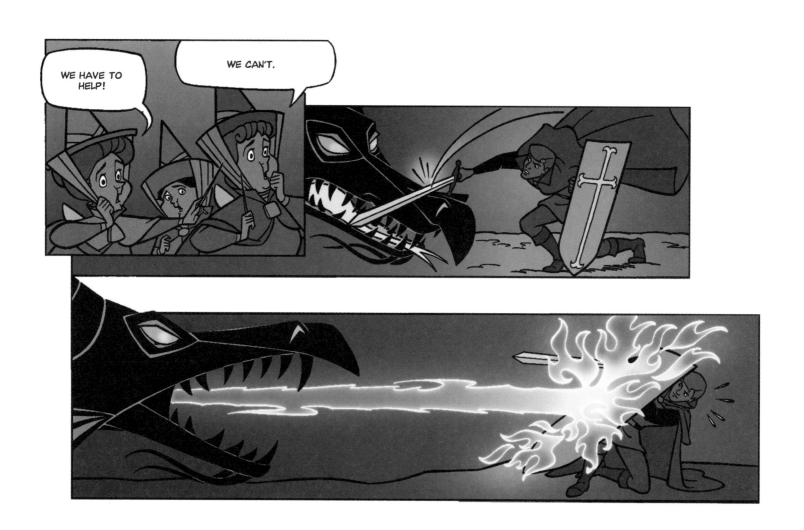

AND, OF COURSE, THE PRINCE HAD ONE OTHER THING.

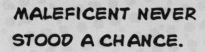

MALEFICENT NEVER STOOD A CHANCE.

ROAR!

NOT AGAINST TRUE LOVE.

FAST AS LIGHTNING THE PRINCE RODE.

AND RAN.

AND CLIMBED.

AND WHEN HE SAW THE PRINCESS ASLEEP... HE KNEW...

...HE'D FOUND HER AGAIN...

...HIS ONE TRUE LOVE.

THE MOMENT THE SLEEPING BEAUTY WAS AWAKENED BY TRUE LOVE'S FIRST KISS, THE REST OF THE KINGDOM WOKE UP AS WELL.

HMM? WHAT WAS I SAYING?

OH, YES. MY SON PHILLIP SAYS HE'S GOING TO MARRY—

MY DAUGHTER AURORA. YES. I KNOW.

WELL, THAT'S THE THING, YOU SEE. PHILLIP'S IN LOVE WITH—

KING HUBERT WASN'T SURE HE UNDERSTOOD WHAT HAD HAPPENED.

AND HE DIDN'T CARE. HIS SON WAS HAPPY—
AND THAT WAS GOOD ENOUGH FOR HIM.

MAY I HAVE
THIS DANCE?

AND WHEN THE HAPPY
COUPLE BEGAN TO DANCE,
THERE WASN'T A DRY EYE
IN THE HOUSE.

190

BLUE OR PINK, IT DIDN'T MATTER.

THE REAL MAGIC WAS THE TRUE LOVE DANCING DOWN BELOW.

AND THEY LIVED HAPPILY EVER AFTER.

THE END